ABUSED

ABANDONED

BUT NOT BROKEN

BY

TARAH BROWN NEWBY

Copyright © 2024 Tarah Brown Newby

CONTENTS

DEDICATION

Have you ever sat and thought about some things you allowed in your life, and you get so angry at yourself? You felt or feel embarrassed, ashamed, defeated? You knew you deserved better, but you still stayed longer than you should have. You look or looked at yourself as a failure because no matter how much you tried; nothing was ever good enough. Well, this book is dedicated to you. Your past is just that - your past. You no longer need to carry that hurt, guilt, or shame of your past.

2 Corinthians 5:17 (NLT) "This means that anyone who belongs to Christ has become a new person. The old life is gone; a new life has begun!

Sure, here's a concise dedication:

For My Sisters, Kathy, Karen, and Kym!

Our bond grew stronger through every challenge, especially after losing our parents. Your love and strength mean the world to me.

I would like to extend my heartfelt thanks to my husband for being so supportive and truly loving me. Your unwavering belief in me has been my anchor. To my children, thank you for pushing me and encouraging me every step of the way. Your inspiration has been my driving force.

ACKNOWLEDGEMENT

Special acknowledgement to my parents, John A. Brown Jr. and Mary F. Brown, your Babygirl did it! I know y'all would be so proud of me.

I would like to send a special thank you to my husband Damion as well as my children, my grandchildren, mother in law Michella, my in-laws, Dr. LaKeya Guy, Tameika Fisher-Moody, Consuella Pinkney, Timotheus "Moe" Peay, DeVeatrice Bryant, and everyone else who took the time to read a chapter/chapters and gave me honest feedback. You are all genuinely appreciated. Thanks so much for your prayers, love, and support through this journey. Thank you

PREFACE

I pray those who read this book don't just read it but my prayer is this helps someone who may be in an abusive/toxic situation/relationship and may feel they are stuck and can't get out for whatever reason. I want you to know that you do not have to settle and there is a way out. Everyone's situation may be different but there's a way out if you're really ready. You are the only one who knows when you have had enough.

Some may not even realize they are in a toxic or abusive relationship. They may say, "Well he/she doesn't hit me, he/she just says mean things to me when I make him/her mad." Hello!!! That's abuse. Verbal abuse can sometimes be more damaging than physical abuse. The wounds/scars can heal over time but words stay with you. You have to go through some work to get through it but the awesome thing is... knowing that You Can! You are Worthy!

This is not a book to bash men or anyone because men also get abused. It's the same for them. My prayer is someone will read my book and realize they don't have to live like that anymore. Leave it to God and I promise He will get you through. People only do what you allow them. I was one of those, it's easier said than done people but guess what? It was done and I'm here to help others!!!
To God, I give all the glory!

CHAPTER 1

The Great Escape

Dear Diary, how did I end up in this mess? I prayed and asked for a good man to come into my life and take away all of the pain from my past. Yes, my past.

When I met Tyrone he was so nice, he paid attention to me, and he complimented me all the time. He would tell me how beautiful I was even when I felt I looked a mess. He always bought me gifts and would send flowers to my job. Everybody loved him. He had everyone sold including me.

It all started to change about 9 months into the relationship. We were out at lunch one afternoon and he brought up the topic of us moving in together. I felt that was not the right thing to do at that time, so I dismissed the idea immediately. The relationship is still pretty fresh in my opinion. He said that he understood where I was coming from and he would wait until I felt comfortable.

We spent most of our days after work together which led to many nights together. When we weren't together, we were always on the phone with each other. Everyone would say how cute we were and tell me how much he was in love with me. I agreed. I was happy. He made me smile. I got butterflies just thinking about him.

It was around Christmas time and at work, we exchanged gifts for our annual polyanna like we have been doing for the past 7 years. Ryan who is a co-worker picked my name, but we were not to disclose who our person was until the day of the holiday party. I received a nice bottle of perfume, a hat, and a glove set (our limit was $50). The gifts were wrapped in a nice box with beautiful wrapping paper, I didn't even want to open it because I loved the wrapping paper.

Tyrone called but I didn't answer the call because I was still at the party, I shot a quick text and said, "Hey honey, I'll call you back, I am in an office party." Tyrone called back again, so I shot another text, "Is everything ok? I'm at work and can't talk right now, I'll hit you back when I can." I put my phone down and continued having fun and enjoying our holiday party.

After 45 minutes, I realized I left my phone at the dessert table, so I went to grab it. There were over 50 missed calls from Tyrone and well over 30 texts accusing me of cheating and messing around with my co-workers behind his back, and threatening to come to my office to confront my male co-workers because I belong to him and nobody takes what's his without a fight and so on and so forth.

I read the messages and I was feeling like "Awwww" he must really love me because he's getting a little jealous. Awwww, this is cute. A side of him that I had never seen before.

So, I excused myself from the party and went into the hallway to call my man and tell him he had nothing to worry about. I'm all his. I dialed his number and he picked up almost immediately.

Tyrone: "I'm telling you now you don't know who you're dealing with.

Me: (laughing) "Baby you don't have to get all worked up. There's nothing going on with me or any of my coworkers. I'm all yours. You're safe."

Tyrone: "Tasha this is not a game. I'll kill for what's mine!"

Me: (still smiling/laughing because he sounded cute) "Awww, babe that's cute, you're getting jealous. Well, I'll call you on my way home from work, love you." I hung up the phone.

Tyrone called me right back but I didn't answer because by then I was gone from the party for quite some time now. I went back to the party and I told my co-worker, Ms. Linda, how Tyrone had been blowing up my phone, how he was showing this jealous side, and how cute that was because he was showing he was really into me. Ms. Linda said, "Be careful T., that could be a red flag." In my head, I'm like, "Of course, she doesn't get it because she doesn't have a man and can't keep one for longer than three months, so she wouldn't understand. Uuugh, she just annoyed me, why did I even say anything to her? She wouldn't understand because she never had a real man who loved her the way Tyrone loves me."

On my way home from work, I got a phone call from my home girl, Kee Kee, wanting to hit up this happy hour spot just to catch up. I said, "ok, cool. I'll be there in 20 mins." We ended up talking until we met up at the spot. Of course, my man called me a few times but I haven't talked or kicked it with any of my girls since Tyrone and I started getting serious, so we needed to catch up.

We were out at the happy hour spot "Teddy's" eating, laughing, drinking, and catching up with my bestie. Tyrone was blowing up my phone, so I answered and he went off yelling and screaming in my ear. So, I stepped away from the table because at this point Kee Kee was looking at me crazy because she could hear him yelling through the phone.

I got back to the table and Kee Kee asked, "What's that all about, T?" I explained the whole situation about him being jealous thinking I was dealing with someone from work and I was supposed to call him on my way home from work (that was my normal routine with him). Kee Kee said, "T, don't you think that's a red flag? " I said to myself, "Oh no, not another hater." Kee Kee was different though because she has a man. I assured her he would get over it and we would be good.

We finished up and I headed home. On my way home, I called Tyrone, no answer. I figured ok, he will call me right back. 10 minutes went by and no call, so I called him again. Still no reply. I guess he fell asleep. No problem then, I can go home unwind, and relax at home, alone.

When I pull up into my driveway, I see Tyrone's car. I'm thinking, "Awwww, this man is the best." I pulled into the driveway and parked next to his black BMW with an all-black interior, slightly tinted windows, and Crome rims with a pinstripe on the side (Yes, my man has a BMW, baby). Anyway, I looked through the windows and he was not in the car. The doors were locked, so he was not in there sleeping, so now, I'm nervous. I called his phone as I was walking through my front door. Still no answer. Now, I'm really nervous. Where is my man? Is he ok? Why is his car here but he's nowhere in sight?

No locks were broken, so I knew he was not in my house. So, I picked up the phone to call my home girl, Kee Kee, to tell her what was going on, and the next thing I knew, I woke up tied to the rails of my bed, naked with a major headache, and Tyrone standing over, top of me. I tried to move my arms but the rope around them was so tight I couldn't do anything.

At this point, I was crying and asking Tyrone what he did to me and why.

He told me he meant what he said when he told me that he plays for keeps. He said, "Game time is over, I'm his forever. The only way out of this is death." In my head, I was wondering, "Who is this man? Where is my loving, sweet, considerate, passionate man that I fell in love with?"

After what seemed like hours of being beaten and raped (It is still rape when you say no and they proceed), he finally cut the rope from my arms and freed me. I tried to run but I was too weak. Besides he wasn't letting me go that easy. He promised if I mentioned anything to anyone ever, he would make sure he killed me.

I took a week off from work and couldn't leave the house because I was bruised so badly, I didn't want anyone to see me and ask questions. After a whole week of being tortured at home, I finally went back to work. The difference now is Tyrone has to take me to and from work. No, going out for lunch with my co-workers like we used to do. Instead, on my lunch break I had to be on the phone with him or he would be at my office waiting for me. I tried to stay that happy positive person so that way nobody would know that deep down inside I was dying. I was crying for help but too scared to tell anyone because no one knew what Tyrone was really capable of.

 One day, out of the blue, my co-worker, Ms. Linda, came to me and said "Tasha, what's going on with you?" I played it off like, "Nothing, girl, what do you mean? I'm good. My man is good, life is great." And she said, "Tasha you need to get away from that man as soon as possible because if not, you're going to end up dead or hurt really bad." I was very offended (on the outside), but on the inside, I was screaming, "Please help me." I told her she had no clue what she was talking about and I told her straight up that she was jealous because I have a good man and she's still single praying to find a man and she shouldn't assume anything about me and my man or it's going to be a problem.

A few more months went by with the same routine. I haven't kicked it with any of my homegirls in months. He convinced me into believing they were hating and wanted him for themselves.

Yippy, it's been a year since me and Tyrone made it official. He had already moved his stuff into my house and set up cameras in every room to monitor my every move as if he wasn't there anyway. Whenever he goes out of the house, he takes my cell phone and unplugs all of the phones in the house. If I tried to go out the door to run to a neighbor the alarm would go off. Same thing if I was stupid enough to try to go through a window to escape.

Tyrone was gone for a few hours, so I did get some relief. When he came into the house, he was so happy and singing, "It's our anniversary." I gave a fake smile and said, " Yup, yes, it is." I guess it wasn't convincing enough because he smacked me dead across my face. Then, he shoved this beautiful 4-carat diamond ring in my face and told me how I don't appreciate him for all he does for me. In my head, I'm like "This man is really crazy because if he thinks beating me every day is what I want for myself, he has no clue." As he puts the ring on my finger, he tells me that we're engaged. He never asked, he just told me that we're getting married.

I go to work the next day and everyone notices the huge ring on my finger but I'm holding back tears. Since our last blow-up at work, I haven't said a word to Ms. Linda and she hasn't said anything to me and I was fine with that. Well, word got around the office that I was getting married and everyone wanted to know the big day, and all of the wedding plans but I had nothing to give them. I wanted no part in this anymore but how do I tell anyone I'm feeling broken? This man who I put up on a peddle stool has been physically, and mentally abusing me on a daily basis!

Two weeks went by and the engagement news died down at work (thank God). I wasn't the topic of the office anymore. I was tired of fake smiling and answering real questions with fake answers. I wasn't myself anymore. I became who Tyrone made me, not who I was ordained to be. Well, I was in the break room, and here comes Ms. Linda. She asked if we could talk for a few minutes. I said, "There's nothing you can or need to say to me." And I walked away. I didn't realize I left my phone on the coffee maker and when I got back to get it, I had eight missed calls from Tyrone! I panicked. I knew what this meant when he came to pick me up. I just started crying, shaking, scared, and lost. I was so lost that I didn't realize Ms. Linda was still sitting in the break room in the corner. She got up and came over to me and just hugged me. She said, "Tasha you have to get out of this situation before it's too late. You can't keep living like this. You have to get out." Right then and there I just gave in. I asked, " How did you know?" She said, "I'd been in an abusive relationship where I stayed with a man for five years because I was weak. I believed he loved me. He treated me well, brought me anything I wanted and even what I didn't want. I was living my best life to the public but inside I was dead" I said, "That's exactly how I feel." She said, "The way you look when he calls you, isn't love, it's panic and fear. You answer every call, he brings you to and from work even when you have your own car. He takes you to the grocery store, he monitors your every move, and he sits across the street from the job all day watching and making sure you're not leaving the door. I know the signs." I said, "Wait, what do you mean he sits across the street from the job?" Ms. Linda said, "Honey when he drops you off at work, he parks across the street facing the front entrance. I see him every single day!" I had no clue. So, I said, "Ms.Linda, can I ask you something? How did you get away? How did you get the courage to just leave?" She said I'd explain later but for now, look out this window and look across the street by that big tree and tell me what you see." Sure enough, it was Tyrone sitting in his all-black BMW, slightly tinted windows, parked with the lights off thinking he was well hidden. Ms. Linda told me to set up for my escape. She said I should start bringing in extra clothes in my work bag with my laptop. She also said I should just pack things in daily and slide them in day by day but make sure he doesn't realize things are missing. She told me to grab all of my important personal documents and anything of value I wanted to make sure I had.

After what seemed like forever; but in reality, it was two months, four days later. Ms. Linda came to me with a straight face and said "Are you sure you're ready for this change?" After the beatdown Tyrone gave me the night before because I questioned him about a female I overheard him talking to. I said, "You bet, I'm ready." Ms. Linda told me there would be a white truck pulling in at the back gate of Garage B to come pick me and my things up at 3 pm sharp. I don't get off until 4 pm, so by the time Tyrone would be looking for me, I would already be at least an hour away.

I had no idea where I was going or what I was going to do about my job, money, my life, or anything. Was Ms. Linda setting me up to get beaten up because of the mean things I said to her? All of these thoughts were going through my mind but you know what? I didn't care. I had to get away and today was my day.

At 2:45, Tyrone called me. That wasn't the normal time for him to call me but he called and I was like, oh no, I knew I shouldn't have trusted Ms. Linda. She set me up! I bet she did. He called and said, "l was just calling to hear your voice." Inside I was feeling mushy like maybe he realized what he was doing and I should give it another try. Well, I guess I was too busy in la la land with my own thoughts that I didn't hear him calling my name. So then, he went back to the mean nasty violent Tyrone and I just said "Ok, baby I'm sorry." The last thing he said to me was "Wait until we get home, this will be the last time you disrespect and ignore me when I'm trying to pour my heart out to your stupid behind." Just the thought of what could happen if I stayed, I looked at the time and it was 2:55 pm. I had 5 minutes to get downstairs to that gate before I missed my escape.

Ms. Linda was right there with me when the truck pulled up, Ms. Linda gave me a huge hug and told me I would be fine and she would be in touch with me shortly. I asked her, "Ms. Linda what do I do? She said, "You don't have to do anything, baby, just thank the Lord and these nice men are going to set you up with everything you need. I'll be in touch with you this evening."

I didn't hesitate. I jumped into the truck while the younger fair-skinned guy grabbed my bags. He handed me a cell phone and said this is your new number and drove me to this beautiful building. The owner of the home was Mrs. Tarah and she showed me around the place. Took me to my room where I would be living for the next six to eight months. She told me not to have any contact with anyone on the outside who's affiliated with Tyrone or that Tyrone has access to.

I was like wait, what is going on here? Then at the same time, I felt free. I had some money in my savings account that Tyrone never knew about because it was in my middle name. I was like ok, I can kick it here and then find a new place. Then I thought about it, why should I have to leave my space because of Tyrone? So now, I'm angry not realizing the blessing.

Ms. Linda kept her word and called me from my "new cell" and told me that Tyrone came in the job looking for me when I didn't come out at 4 like I normally do. I was so wrapped up in my thoughts I didn't realize that my "old phone" didn't even ring. Ms. Linda had my service shut off, and my things in my house were in a storage under an alias name. She spoke to HR at my job, so I was able to keep my job but work from the house until I moved to a different state. I chose to move to another state because I didn't want to take any chances running into Tyrone ever again in life.

To this day, I keep in contact with Ms. Linda and Mrs. Tarah. I have no clue what happened to Tyrone and I care less. I moved to Florida about two and a half years ago, brought a 3 bedroom condo and I am engaged to an awesome man who loves the Lord and loves me. I am so thankful for Mrs. Tarah. We all need a Ms. Linda in our lives.

CHAPTER 2

Dear Diary 1

Dear Diary, It has been two years and four months since I last saw Larry. He's been writing me letters, blowing my phone up, and sending messages through mutual friends. I changed my number several times but somehow he ended up getting it and calling. I haven't returned any of his letters and don't plan on doing so at all or answering his calls. I definitely will not be taking that five-hour trip to the prison to visit him, so I wish he would just leave me alone and move on with his life because I sure did.

I don't know how or why but I allowed Trina and Rachel to talk me into checking out this new "hot spot" that just opened up downtown. The entire time I was looking through my closet trying to figure out what to wear but I was also trying to talk myself out of going. I can't just lock my door and lay on the couch and act like I fell asleep because they both have keys to my house and I know they will pop right on up over here and put my clothes on me and make me go.

Uuuugh, who am I fooling? They aren't going to let it rest until I go, so I might as well suck it up, get dressed and get it over with. I'll pretend like I'm having a good time. I may stay out for an hour or two but definitely no longer than that. Besides, I am a little hungry so I'll grab a bite to eat. I hear they have some really good wings. Hmmmm now this sounds like a plan!

We planned to meet up at 7 pm but course of, Rachel was late as usual and we didn't get seated until 7:45 pm. It was a really nice upscale grown folk spot. It was like a fancy lounge. It had the most beautiful light fixtures. There was a live band playing some good ole oldies, they had a separate area if you wanted to have a private room. Pretty much like a VIP area! It was very classy. I was impressed.

The music was lively. The band was playing that grown and sexy R & B Soul for real music. I was sipping on a glass of some sweet red wine and actually was enjoying being out.

I was interrupted by a tap on my shoulder. I turned around and there stood the finest man I had ever seen in my life. I mean this man was finer than fine. He was about 6'4 caramel complexion, stocky built, and honey, with broad shoulders and, a nice beard that was perfect for his brown bald shining head. He had on black jeans, a white button-up shirt, a black blazer, and a polka dot printed pocket square.

And honey, when he sat down his socks matched his pocket square!!! His scent, baby, let me tell you... I don't know what he was wearing but it caught everyone's attention especially mine!

"Hello ladies, my name is Rashan. Do you ladies mind if I buy you all a drink?" Rachel is the outspoken one in the crew so she spoke first and said "OK OK! I see you out here looking and acting like a grown man, I like that." Trina immediately cut her off because if you know Rachel, she will say whatever is on her mind and that isn't always good. Trina says, "Thank you sir that's kind of you, we will have three glasses of Caymus. Thank you."

I was sitting there watching my two besties flirt and gawk at this man who is fine and all of that but don't get it twisted; after all the crap I have been through, all I'm trying to do is get some wings, wine and take my butt back home to my bed, ALONE! Rashan says to me (in the midst of my besties acting like groupies) "Are you always this quiet or is it you just sitting back and observing?" I said "I'm not quiet, I'm very laid back, no drama, no bull crap type of female, that's all. I guess I'm not thirsty if that makes sense." Well, apparently he liked that comment because the next thing I know two hours went by and we were still there tearing them good ole spicy, honey and sweet and chili wings up.

Trina and Rachel wore themselves out on that dance floor.

When I tell you that live band was jumping. They went from Usher's "My Boo" to New Editions, "Lost in Love." I mean they were jamming. Just as we were heading towards the exit, Rashan grabbed my hand, took my cell phone, and put his number in my phone. I thought that was corny but cute.

I didn't want to seem desperate so I waited a few days before calling. We decided to meet up and we had brunch. On about our fifth or sixth date, I felt things were moving a little too fast but I didn't care. I was finally smiling and happy again. My girls were excited that I was excited. I was living my best life.... so I thought.

About three months went by and things between me and Rashan are still hot and heavy. We're together almost every day. The letters from Larry completely stopped and I was so happy about that, so I decided not to mention anything about Larry to Rashan. I mean what's the point? Larry was in my past and locked up for God knows how long, so why mention him? No need to stir up any drama.

As I am sitting in my newly repainted lavender, yellow, and white decorated bedroom, folding clothes and listening to some good ole old-school music, my doorbell rings. I looked out the bedroom window but I didn't see anyone. What I did see were five balloons that said, "You're special, Thinking of You, #1 Fan with the finger up, Boss Baby and an I love you balloon filled with money along with a teddy bear attached. I looked around and didn't see Rashan's truck anywhere but he likes to surprise me, so I didn't think anything of it. The balloons were very thoughtful but that "I love you" one caught me off guard. I was like, "Oh yeah, he's tripping. I mean he's cool and all but love?" We are not ready for that. I know I'm not but I do care about him. He's been consistent with showing me who he is daily. He hasn't switched up on me yet.

I called Rashan to thank him for the beautiful balloons, but he did not answer. That's not like him so I figured he must be sleeping.

About thirty minutes later, Rashan called me back, and instead of me mentioning the balloons and bear because it slipped my mind, we made plans to hook up later that evening.

It's three hours later and I'm fresh out of the shower ready for my dinner date with my new man. Well wait, is he my man because at this point we haven't made anything official between us yet. We're simply enjoying each other's presence that's why the "I love you" balloon threw me off.

I left the door unlocked because I knew Rashan was on his way and I was still getting myself ready. This is nothing new, we've done it plenty of times before.

I ran down to the kitchen to grab a glass of water then I heard the doorbell. I yell out, "Come on in, Bae." To my surprise, it's not Rashan at all. In fact, it's Larry! He has this crazy creepy look on his face and his eyes look red and full of anger. He sees my ballons and Bear and smirks and says "Oh I see you like my gift huh?" I could not speak. It's like I had a frog stuck in my throat.

As Larry was coming towards me, I tried to run to the back door but he was right on it. He knew me!

He grabbed me by my neck and started choking me to the point I was having trouble breathing. As much as I was fighting him back, he was not letting loose. He must have felt my body getting weak and limp, so he let me go and told me that it was too easy for him to kill me, I had to suffer for sending him to jail, not responding to his letters, and blocking all of his calls. I still could not respond to anything he was asking me. I was just praying he would realize I'm not worth it and just leave and let me live.

After being beaten up for what felt like hours. There was a knock on my door. I knew it had to be Rashan. I didn't know what to do because I did not want to drag this man into my old drama that he knew nothing about but on the other hand, I wanted to live. Without realizing it, I screamed at the top of my lungs, "Help me please, help me!! Call 911, Please hurry."

Rashan came running to my kitchen and saw Larry on top of me about to strike me in the face and that's when Rashan threw him off of me and began to beat him down. I was trying to gather myself and get to my phone to call the police and all of a sudden I heard two gunshots! BOOM BOOM!!!

I was so terrified to turn around but when I did, my heart dropped to the ground. Rashan was shot! Larry was charging towards me and out of the corner of my eye I saw my favorite knife in the dish rack. As he was charging towards me, I grabbed the knife and just started swinging and accidentally stabbed Larry. Larry went down to the ground. I kept the knife in my hand and ran over to both men down on the ground and called 911 then I ran over to Rashan. He was still breathing, thank God.

I called my neighbor Denise and told her I needed help so she and her husband David came over and stayed with me until the police and ambulance arrived.

God is so good! Only one of the bullets hit Rashan on his left side. The other just barely grazed him.

As for Larry, he was in ICU for two weeks and once released, he was sent back to state prison to serve a 10-15 year sentence with no parole!

Thankfully, Rashan forgave me for not letting him know what was going on and we made a vow to always be open and honest with each other no matter what the situation was.

What I learned from this experience was to make sure to completely close one door before opening another one. This could have gone a whole other way quickly!

CHAPTER 3

Dear Diary 2

Sitting on the freshly bleached bathroom floor in my one-bedroom apartment, a pregnancy test from the Rite Aid in my hand, and tears running down my face. "This cannot be happening. Please, God, don't let this be true. Not right now. I was just planning my getaway and now this? Why God? Why now? Please help me!!!"

Just when I thought I had things planned and my escape in progress, I had to end up pregnant. "Can it get any worse than this? What am I going to do now?" I've never had an abortion before but I can't have this man's baby. He will never leave me alone then I'll be stuck with him for the rest of my life. I have to come up with a plan B.

I went from sitting on the bathroom floor to sitting on the edge of my pearly white toilet. "Huuuum, maybe I'll just move away and never tell him anything about the baby. Or how about I have the baby and just give it up for adoption or something?" I don't know but I have to figure it out and soon. On the flip side, who knows, maybe if I tell him I'm pregnant, he can be happy and will stop taking his anger out on me.

Dear diary,

It's been a few weeks and I still haven't told Raymond I was pregnant. I'm not sure what I'm going to do yet. Do I run away? But where will I go? Wherever I decide to go, I'm sure he will find me. He reminded me of that quite often.

So much on my mind. I can't have this baby. Lord, please help me. I don't know what to do. I don't want to get attached to this baby because it's a part of him and I really want to be done with him once and for all. I have to think quickly. Time is ticking and this baby is only growing and developing inside me. I refuse to abort it but I feel if I keep this baby, I will never be able to get away. The only thing I can think of that makes any sense is to figure out a way to lose this baby. This is my only option at this point!!

Dear diary,

Today is February 3rd, the day I will finally tell Raymond we are expecting. I really hope he's happy.

Dinner was cooked, the house was clean, and trash was taken out so there should be no reason for us not to have a good night.

As soon as Ray walked through the door, I knew something was wrong. I fixed his plate and we sat down to eat dinner. While we were having dinner, his phone was blowing up. He looked at it and kept eating (woofing his food down like he hadn't eaten in weeks). His phone went off again and I asked, "Aren't you going to answer your phone? Apparently, someone is trying to get your attention" Next thing I know, I was smacked straight across my face.

At that moment, I knew I could not tell him about this baby. Raymond left the house without saying a word to me. I made up my mind I couldn't have this baby. I had to get rid of it by any means necessary. I went to my closet where I had my secret stash and began drinking. I drank a whole bottle of hard liquor straight hoping I would pass out and wake up and the baby would be gone and all of this will just be a horrible dream. It didn't work out the way I planned.

Although I did pass out, apparently because it was the next day when I finally got up. Raymond was nowhere to be found. I called his phone and no answer so I went back to my stash again and drank until I couldn't take anymore. Still nothing. No bleeding from a miscarriage, no bad pains or cramping in my belly like Google said it would be. Well, maybe I didn't drink enough. This went on for a few more weeks. Drinking every night until I passed out. Raymond didn't even notice.

I didn't know what to do next so I wrote my best friend who lived miles away. I told her my situation and asked if I could come and stay with her until I figured out what was my next move. Let's just say, I never made it to Alabama. Raymond found the letter and beat me so badly for not telling him I was pregnant and an extra beat down for thinking about leaving him. At this point, I had no choice but to keep the baby.

Dear diary,

This first trimester is very rough for me. Morning sickness, headaches, and no appetite. The Doctors are concerned because I'm losing too much weight and I'm already skinny. What can I do?

Dear diary,

Raymond was excited that we were having a baby. Things were getting better. I was actually excited about being pregnant. Mentally, I wasn't ready to be a mom but I had no choice. I had to get it right because one thing was for sure, I was pregnant and the baby was coming whether I was ready or not.

Dear diary,

I'm in my Third trimester now and I'm so ready to have this baby. I feel like a balloon that's about to pop. Raymond hasn't been around much which was fine with me so that means less beatings but if he's not home, where is he? There has to be someone else. When I ask, he tells me he's just out in the streets hanging on the block. He pays the bills so I don't question him too much besides the house was peaceful, so why mess it up?

Later that night, I got a call that Raymond was out with another female. I went outside to confront him in front of this girl. She knows we're having a baby and she knows he's my man, so yes, I'm going to confront both of them. As I'm walking to find him, he's actually on his way home.

I confront him and ask him about this girl and of course he denies it and everything else. Things got heated as we were walking home and the next thing I knew, I was being dragged up the street. When someone in a car rode past and asked what was going on, he said I fell and he was helping me up. By the time I got home, thank God we were only a block or two away, there was blood everywhere. I had no clue where the blood was coming from because my entire 7-month pregnant ole body was numb.

Raymond got me in the house and ran me a bath water and told me to clean myself up. He demanded that I stop crying but I was in so much pain, I couldn't. That's when he smacked me so hard, hit me in my head, and when I bent down and began to hold my belly to protect the baby I was carrying, he began to kick me which led to him stomping me while I was in a ball still trying to protect our unborn child who I began to love and was excited to meet. His excuse was that I made him do it because of my smart mouth! Wow! I get stomped and beaten like a man in the street because of my mouth? This can't be what life is. Jesus, help me get out of this, please.

Dear diary,

Today, I delivered a baby girl. She is beautiful. I did it! She is perfect. Raymond was so excited and today was perfect in spite of her being premature. I can't ask for a better gift. A gift of life. Now, things have to get better from here. Raymond has a daughter now, so hopefully this will calm him down. "Wow, I finally have a family, " I said to myself. "This is going to be great! Thank you Jesus for my family and not having to go through with my plan B!"

Just when I thought things would get better, it only got worse. Some nights, Raymond wouldn't even come home and the nights he did come home he was always so drunk and violent. I dreaded when I heard the car pulling into the driveway.

After going through this for so long, my life, mind, and body were just so numb. I didn't love Raymond anymore. I was starting to build very ill feelings towards and about him. Thinking about him made me feel things inside of me that I knew weren't right.

I couldn't go on living like this. I want better. I have a daughter now who will be looking at and watching my moves. I wanted better for her so I knew I had to make some major decisions in my life.

One day, while I was sitting in my bedroom putting my precious pride and joy down for a nap, I started thinking about my grandmom. She was very petite and soft-spoken but when she spoke, her words were stern and with so much love. Boy, I miss her. She was such a wise woman who loved the Lord.

Out of nowhere, it just hit me...All of this time I've been feeling so lost, down, oppressed, and felt like giving up but I couldn't. My grandmom although she's not with me physically, I still hear her voice reminding me that " I am fearfully and wonderfully made" (Psalms 139: 14)I am a King's daughter! "l can do all things through Christ who strengthens me!!"(Philippians 4:1 3)

One of my favorite scriptures is Jeremiah 29: 11"For I know the plans I have for you," declares the Lord. Plans to prosper you and not harm you. Plans to give you hope and a future. "

From that day on, I made up my mind that I would not be a victim any longer. I had to make some life-changing decisions for me and my daughter. I called my best friend and told her I was ready. (She always told me I would know when I was really ready to leave Raymond) Well, I was ready to leave his trifling behind right where he belonged (to the streets).

My bestie called her cousin and his crew. We headed to the home that Raymond and I shared and packed all of our belongings. That was the beginning of a great new life for me and my baby girl.

CHAPTER 4

Mom's Dukes: A Son's Struggle

Ever since I was a child, my mom trained us on how to steal so I don't understand why she was surprised when I got my first charge at thirteen years old. I was just doing what I saw and what I was taught.

Mom Dukes used to take me and my little sisters to the stores and would steal anything she could fit inside our pants, jackets, pockets even down to our socks. That's not even including the things she had on her. When I was old enough to go to the stores on my own, what do you think I did? I did what I was taught. What Moms didn't teach us was if you get caught, you go to jail. She taught us how not to get caught.

This time, I did not follow the rules Moms laid out for us and was greedy. Man, I was almost out the door, but I remembered when I was in the check-out line that I never copped that lighter I saw. I went to grab it but saw it was $5, so I said I could shoot to the dollar store that's right next door. I was not paying $5 for no lighter. Nah, that's not happening. So, I went back. If only I had just walked out those doors, I would have gotten away.

Growing up, I was raised with both parents. Mom's real name is Darleen Marie Barks (Barnes).

If I was asked as a child to describe my Mom, I would say she was an angry woman who had children at a young age and blamed her children for the decisions/choices she made.

As an adult, looking back, I realize Moms was showing love the way she knew how. She is what my Pops called a stallion. Moms stood 5'9 dark skin, thick built, shortcut, and loud!

Outside the house, Moms was highly respected and well-known. My grandma was a bartender for one of the top bars in town. She knew everybody and she made sure everybody knew her and our family. She loves her family so much. I cannot recall Moms ever having a job, she said Momma G (Gina) taught her from a little girl to find a man who works and will take care of her; and that's exactly what she did.

Momma G played a huge part in our lives. It was cool having her come over but sometimes it was too much because even as a young man, she was too raw and blunt, and I felt she had no respect for men. That's how she raised Moms and my Aunties. Since I was there, the only boy in the house, Momma G made sure Mom Dukes stayed on me. She told my Moms to make sure she taught me how to be a real man! Even though I was a young boy in my head. I was asking myself, "Why is a woman teaching me how to be a man when my dad who is a man is right here?" I just did not understand that, but I wouldn't dare ask the question. Moms taught us not to question her or what she does (including my Dad).

My little sister, Rain, bumped her head one day. She snapped and asked Moms why she didn't want to go out and get a job like normal Moms do, instead of having her kids go out to steal. Man, Moms lost it. She asked no questions; she went and grabbed her favorite belt and started using it on Rain!! My sister Angel, wanted to go in there and help her, but what could we do? We just waited until Mom's arm got tired, and she sent Rain out of the room. When Rain got into the room with us, her face was dry and balled up, but she had no tears, no emotions, no nothing! Meanwhile, Angel was in their room with crocodile tears running down her face imagining the pain Rain was going through. I am doing my best to hold it together because if Moms caught me crying, I would be next.

She told me, "Real men don't cry, only chumps do, and we don't have chumps in our bloodline." Moms stood on that!

My dad, Anthony Barnes Sr., worked in construction. He was a part of the local union for over 25 years. My Dad would get up every morning, leave the house when it was still dark, and get home around 5:30 pm. We watched my dad get up and make his breakfast and pack his lunch every day while Moms laid around giving out orders.

My dad was the oldest of 4 siblings. My Dad was like a giant. He stood 6 feet 3 inches and weighed about 320 lb, all solid. He is fit and in great shape. I can't say he eats the healthiest but because he is so active, it looks like he works out. Moms hated that Dad was a handsome man and before Moms scooped him up, he was a ladies' man. Grandma Betty was the total opposite of Momma G. Ma Betty is what she let us call her. When she came around it was always love, hugs, smiles, and laughter. Hearing stories about my parents and how they grew up was always interesting. Their backgrounds were the same as far as growing up in the same area, went to the same schools, shopped at the same stores but lived totally opposite. Ma Betty raised her children in the church, and she would stay on Dad telling him he needed to get back into the church. She would say, "The Lord is coming soon and you don't want to be left behind, so get them kids into a good God-fearing church, son. It's your responsibility as a man!" This conversation came up often and Dad just shook his head in agreement. In his defense, whenever Dad mentions anything about church, Moms shuts down the idea immediately.

If I were asked to describe my Dad, and how it was growing up in a house with him, I would say, he was always a great provider, hard worker, loving, faithful, and fun (when Moms was not around). But as an adult, looking back, the word that comes to mind is...Stuck!

When I was thirteen years old, I got busted for stealing. They put me in the back of that police car, and I knew right then I was in for it! Not for stealing but for getting caught! Before they took me to the police station for my parents to come pick me up, they took me into this room where it had cameras all over, showing videos of me stealing. They were impressed at how I was able to get so many items and looking at me, you could not tell I had anything on me. Like I said, what gave it away was me going back to grab that lighter I saw at the register. I needed that lighter because I bought a loosey one from one of the old heads on the block for a dollar.

Smoking helped me calm my nerves and all the old heads out there were doing it, so hey, why not? For my first offense, in my head I'm thinking I'll be right back at home, I won't come back to this store for a few months and then I'll be back to hit them up like I have been doing. Well, that's not what happened. I was put in what they call a juvenile detention center with a group of boys who got in trouble. I was there for six months. Being there around a group of kids who did bad things for fun was not who I was. To me, I wasn't bad like some of the boys I met while in that place. I just stole not because I wanted to but because I had to. There's a difference.

This place was called YAMIND (Young Adult Men In New Direction). I was not a young adult, I was thirteen. I had five years before I turned eighteen. I did not belong there. Mr. D, the owner of the whole facility, was cool and he seemed to care about the youth in the community. The facility was huge but Dr. D always came to inspect the facility to make sure everywhere was clean.

At thirteen, I did not understand what was going on. I was scared but I wouldn't dare show it. After a few days, I got used to the environment. Adapting to the staff and the kids was not so hard. I was able to complete 7th grade while I was there. What started out as a bad situation helped build me to be the man I am today. I met a few kids who also did not belong there but what we realized later in life is that we were supposed to be there! When I completed the program at YAMIND, I passed to go to the 8th grade. They had a little graduation ceremony for those who were eligible. It was fly.

The hardest part of the entire program was not getting a visit from Moms, Dad, and my sisters. Even Ma Betty and Grandpa Jim took that hike to come visit me. Moms felt it was all my fault and she didn't want to be a part of it. She said I got that scariness from my Dad's side because there's nothing soft about her side. I wanted to say, "That's the problem" but I wanted my teeth, so I stayed humble.

Things were different at home because I got caught stealing. Moms would not let that go! I had about a week and a half to enjoy the summer before going back to school. I told her I didn't want to steal anymore, I told her when I turned fifteen, I would get a job and help financially, so we wouldn't have to steal anymore. Man, why did I say that? Moms went ham on me.

She felt that was an insult and suggested I was saying we were poor and needed a handout. I just never understood why we had to steal because Dad had a decent job. We never went without lights and water, and we always had plenty of food. I just never understood why Dad didn't put his foot down or choose to leave.

She would always yell, saying, "Your dad goes out here working his behind off to take care of y'all ungrateful tails and y'all don't appreciate none of it!" While she was going on with her rant, Angel, Rain and I gave each other that look because we knew the drama was about to start. The manipulation of how much she sacrificed by having us. She could have put us all up for adoption, but she didn't. She kept us and made sure we had the best of everything... yeah we know. It is always somebody else's fault. We've heard her say this too often that can even mimic but of course, in our heads.

Ok, so fast forward to when I graduated from high school with a 3.8 GPA. Getting into a good college would have been a smooth ride for me. I kept in contact with Mr. D from YAMIND and he told me he would hook me up with a job when I got out and he kept his promise. For that, I am thankful.

When Rain turned eighteen, Dad took us out to eat and he told us that he was sorry, but he could not take the abuse from Moms anymore and he was leaving. He gave us the option to come with him or to stay with Moms, but he was out. We had no clue why he decided to do it on Rain's eighteenth birthday. He said he only stayed around for us. He didn't want us to be raised in a broken home because that's not how he was raised. He apologized for breaking up the family, but he had enough of Moms tearing him down, so he was out. I must be honest. I think his leaving was one of the best decisions he made.

With Dad out of the house, the girls started smelling themselves as Moms would say (the girls started to become more confident) but she continued trying to control, manipulate, and mentally abuse them. My sisters couldn't take it anymore, so they packed their stuff and moved in with Dad. I was happy they got out but then it was only me and Moms in the house.

You would think, with her husband leaving and now her daughters gone, she would at least stop and think, "Hey, could there be something going on with me that is pushing everybody away?" Instead, she somehow turned this all on Dad. Saying how Ma Betty kept her titty in Dad's mouth for too long and that's why he doesn't know how to be a man. He was only good at providing and in bed. "Who wants to hear how about their parent's sex life right?" Well, that is another thing Moms had no shame about.

She taught me how to use and manipulate girls to get them to do exactly what I needed them to do and when I needed it done. It worked. I had women fighting over me to prove their love and devotion to me. Moms would sit back and be so proud when the women went at it. Especially, when they would call her. She enjoyed seeing these females hurting by my actions but at the same time, she was tearing me down at the same time.

My friends loved Moms. She even taught them the same thing. She felt she was helping them out because they didn't grow up with daddies in the house and their Mom was too bougie and weak to teach them how to be men. She felt it was her duty as a good-hearted woman to help these weak boys become men (her words). My friends saw it as an opportunity, but in reality, we were hurting other people's feelings, and emotions and we also took their money. Some of them have kids. I want out but what am I supposed to do? Everybody else left Moms, so I am all she has right now.

One day, Moms asked if I could take her to the mall real quick to grab a few things. She was going out with Ms. Shar, later. It was cool because I didn't have any plans until that night with a girl whom I had been developing feelings for.

While at the mall with Moms, I decided to check out some Polos, so I asked Moms to watch my jacket while I tried them on. When I came out of the dressing room she was gone and a guy at the mall said, "Hey Homie, your Moms said you should meet her at the car." I didn't think anything of it because that was normal for Moms because she did not like being out long.

As I walked towards the food court exit, I saw two police officers and I heard Moms cussing and fussing. I ran to find out what was going on. One of the police officers grabbed me and instantly tried to take me to the ground. I had no clue what was going on, but Moms started going off on everybody. Before you know it, we are at the precinct getting fingerprinted and charged with shoplifting, resisting arrest, assault, and a few other charges.

Even though I wasn't involved in what happened, because of my police contact, which was a school violation, and they were very strict about their rules and regulations, I lost my full academic scholarship. One thing is for sure, Dad and Mr. D never gave up on me and believed in me even when I was ready to give up on myself.

Mr. D had a business partner named Jon T. who looked out for me. I was working at Sheild Engineering as one of the top Engineers. I was doing pretty good for myself, but I still felt disconnected. It's like something was missing but I did not know what it was.

Dad called me one Saturday night and told me he needed to see my face in church that Sunday. Although I didn't live under my Dad's roof, I still respected him and wouldn't dare talk back. I told him I would come to church that Sunday and that's just what I did. I haven't stepped foot in a church in over fifteen years at this point. Moms came at me every time I mentioned church or when she would see me dressed up to go out, she made comments about me trying to be like my dad who she thinks was being brainwashed by his bougie family. I wasn't going to let her stop me this time. I gave Dad my word. What I did not know was that I was in for a WORD! It was crazy because as an adult, walking through those doors, it took me back to when I was a little boy. I really wanted to play the guitar and the drums but when I told Moms, she said she wasn't raising a choir boy, so I never mentioned it again.

The whole service seemed like it was for me. The Usher welcomed me and led me right to the front where my Dad and siblings were seated.

As I was taking my seat, they called this brother up to bless the congregation with a selection. When this man opened his mouth, it was like what the old folks used to say, "He has the voice of an angel" The words just flowed out: "Here I am struggling, fighting a battle in my mind. I'm trying to control all the changes and tests of time. I've been crying out for so long, but no one seems to understand. Some people call me crazy, but I say I'm just a man" Then, he hit us with the "We all have struggles, we all have problems, we all have situations, but we can't let them control us." By the time he got to the next hook, he had the congregation going crazy. I was feeling it, but you know me, I'm too cool for all of that. There were beautiful ladies in the church too, so I had to keep cool. Moms didn't raise a chump.

Well, that's what I was trying to convince myself of. When this man went into the next hook and said: "l cannot judge all the things that you do. But don't put me down, I'm only like you. There are some things in my life that can't seem to change. Our problems may be different but to God, we're the same. Because we all have struggles, we all have problems, we all have situations that we can't control."

Next thing I know, I'm on my knees surrendering and giving my life to Christ. From that day forward, God made me a new man.

Moms still hasn't changed her ways but as for me and my household, we serve the Lord.

My name is Anthony Barnes Jr, and I am a survivor of psychological abuse.

CHAPTER 5

Staying In A Child's Place:

A Daughter's Cry

Being a child is so hard sometimes. Grown-ups tell you what and what not to do but they do the very things they teach you not to do. Then have the nerve to tell you, " Do as I say not as I do!" The famous one my parents always told me and my younger sister was "What goes on in this house, stays in this house. We don't need anybody meddling in our business" What I took from that was…don't tell anybody how my daddy would come home drunk as a skunk and beat you up, breaking all our stuff and then going on and on ranting about how he paid for it, so he can do what he darn well please. It's his house, he's the king of this castle. Whoever doesn't like it, should pack their bags and leave because this is his house, blah blah blah!

This wasn't an everyday thing but it happened enough. Too much if you ask me but what do I know? I'm only a kid, right? I don't understand grown folks. I guess that's why I was always told to stay in a child's place. Even as a child, I knew that's not what I wanted for myself or my baby sister.

When Mama found out she was pregnant with my baby sister, Tabitha (Tabbie), Daddy was not happy about that. He accused her of sleeping around behind his back, despite knowing that Mama did not go anywhere without him knowing. He had a tracker on everything, so he could see whatever he needed to see. When Mama got a call or when my Auntie would text Mama's phone, Daddy could see it on some fancy iPad tablet that he kept to monitor her every move.

I often wondered if Mama ever asked if she could track his whereabouts too but I doubt it because Mama never stood up for herself and plus I did not want to get popped in my mouth for being in grown folk's business, so I would just vent to Tabbie.

The day I laid eyes on my baby sister, I knew from that day that I had a responsibility to protect her. She was born prematurely which I later found out means she was born a little earlier than the doctors wanted and expected but she was perfect in my eyes. Tabbie had the brightest hazel brown eyes I've ever seen. Her skin was pale and wrinkled. She had a head full of curly hair and she was super long. The Doctor said she was going to be a basketball player because she was so long. Whatever she was destined to be I just knew I wanted to protect her, just like how my Aunt Tee always tried to protect Mama especially, from my Daddy.

Things got so bad that Daddy would take me and Tabbie on play dates with other women's kids and give us ice cream or buy us new toys, so we wouldn't mention it to Mommy. I never told her because I felt she already knew what he was out there doing but she still allowed him to come and go as he pleased, so I did what I felt was best and that was to stay in a child's place.

I remember sitting in the closet in our bedroom with the door closed, holding Tabitha's hands over her ears and both of us humming, trying to block out all the mean, nasty names and things Daddy was saying to and about Mama.

This went on for so Iong that we outgrew the small closet space. Then we started switching beds, depending on who jumped in who's bed first. That's where we end up holding each other promising that we will never be weak like our Mommy and we vowed to never allow a man who says they love us to treat and talk to us any kind of way.

Aunt Tee put me and Tabbie in some youth program at her church and we learned so much about God, life, how we are supposed to live as Christians and so much more. That was the most excitement we had because Daddy did not allow us to sign up for any after-school activities, the local cheer teams, not even Girl Scouts, he said he didn't want any other man looking at his girls. I didn't understand how he could say that out of his mouth but he was out here running these streets with at least three other women that Mommy knew about. But hey, I'm just a child so I'm staying in a child's place.

Going to Aunt Tee's church got Mama a little break from Daddy. He only allowed her to go because he said he didn't want to hear my Aunt Tee's mouth. My Auntie does not play!

I guess from Mama sitting up under that good word (as I hear the older church folks say) did something to her because after a while Mama started looking happy. The only time we got to see her smile and actually enjoy herself is when she gets to spend time with me and Tabbie alone or when Aunt Tee comes around and takes us to church with her. Other than that, Mama looks so sad and so defeated. Probably because Daddy always has her up doing stuff that he should be doing himself. But I wouldn't dare say that out loud but only to Tabbie because we knew to stay in a child's place.

Daddy came into the house one evening after staying out all night again but he wasn't drunk this time. He came into the house and just started ranting on and on, complaining about everything he could think of, as usual.

Well, this time was different. Mama did not have that defeated look on her face as she normally does when Daddy starts with her. This time she looked different! It actually looked like she was smiling.

Apparently, Daddy felt the same way because before we knew it, whoop right across her face with his backhand. Out of nowhere, Tabitha jumps up and yells, "Satan I rebuke you in the name of Jesus!" Boy, oh boy! I thought for sure Tabbie was gonna get the whopping of her life but instead, Daddy turned and looked at Ma and said, "l see what you're doing, you're trying to turn my girls against me but that's not going to happen. I'll take you out of here before I let you take them from me. I've got plenty of women who would kill to be in your shoes but you're too stupid to realize that! You can't do anything without me. You'll never be anything. I made you girl and don't ever forget that!" Mama didn't say a word, she just smiled and told me and my little sister it was time to shower and prepare for bed.

The next morning, we were getting up for school and Mama came into our room, she had a very serious look on her face so we knew something was going on. Concerned, we asked her if everything was ok.

Then, Aunt Tee came into the house just as cheerful and smiling as usual, so now, we're really concerned. They sat us down and explained that Mama was going to leave Daddy and we had to go to a different school and we wouldn't contact our friends or Daddy.

We were actually happy that she was finally leaving him. After we packed up as much of our stuff as we could. We thought we were going to be living with Aunt Tee and Uncle Joe but instead, we ended up in this beautiful place that was shared with other families but each family had their own room. Everyone there was so friendly. When I say this place had anything you could ask for that was an understatement.

I later found out this place was called WIND (Women In New Direction) which is a transitional home for battered women.

I thank God for sending us to this place because it really helped Mama out big time. We were only there for six months. They helped Mama find a job and we were able to move into our own 3-bedroom home where we had our own space. Tabitha and I were able to transfer to new schools and we met some really great friends, best of all Mama was happy. We missed our Daddy but didn't miss how he treated Mommy.

Once Mama divorced Daddy and felt comfortable, she let us call Daddy but we were not allowed to tell him where we were. All he wanted to know was if Mommy had us around any other men. That was always his biggest concern. Not how we were doing, he didn't even ask if we were in school or if we needed anything!

I wanted to tell him how much we loved our new home, how big Tabbie's and my room was, and how happy Mama was making her own money, being free to come and go as she pleased, and just soooo much but I wouldn't dare do that. That wouldn't be staying in a child's place and I knew better than that!

Now that I am grown with a family of my own, I got the nerve to ask my Mama why she allowed Daddy to treat her the way he did and for so long. I didn't know how to come out and ask with tears pouring from my eyes. I asked, "Mama, I know I've always been told to stay in a child's place but where is that place? As a child I watched you tolerate and deal with a man who said he loved you but he kept beating and tearing you down. He humiliated you and you never stood up for yourself! You took it and did not fight back. Why were you so weak, Mama? Why didn't you stand up for yourself?"

Her response was, "You're right baby. I was weak. I stayed because I felt I needed him. I tried to make a family for you and your little sister. I made excuses for his behavior because he wasn't raised with a father and I felt it wasn't his fault! I allowed everything because I felt I needed him. We needed him but we didn't! I am so sorry baby."

I told her we forgave her, we just didn't understand but one thing was for sure Tabitha and I made a vow as little kids that we would not allow anyone to treat us any kind of way because we are God's children so anyone who dealt with us had to handle us with care.

We had many breakups and slip-ups in life but we kept our vow and we both are happily married with our own children.

Mama is happily married to a man of God named Mr. Melvin who treats Mama like the Queen she is, while Daddy is still out there running around sleeping and beating on every woman that allows it but that's his business, I'm grown and still staying in a child's place.

CHAPTER 6

Confronting My Abuser

It's been fifteen years since I have seen or heard anything from or about Preston King and I could have gone the rest of my life without seeing or hearing his name again.

"Hello, Mrs. King. How are you? My name is Levi Brown and I'll be representing your husband Preston. I just wanted to come and introduce myself to you. I was hoping to meet your lovely daughter."

"Excuse me? Mrs. King?? Sorry sir, you must have me mixed up with someone else. I am not Mrs. King and haven't been for over fourteen years, so please don't ever make that mistake again. Thank you, now if you'll excuse me, I have a life to move on with.. have a blessed day." I politely walked away and took my seat waiting and praying this case would be short, sweet, and finally over.

I was sitting in my seat waiting for the Honorable Judge Wilko to arrive, and out of nowhere I felt this sudden feeling of anxiety rush through my body, my hands started sweating, my heart started beating super fast, and my ears were ringing. It's like everything was happening so fast. I had to get some water. I had to get out of there and quickly without making a scene. As I got up to walk, my legs buckled but I grabbed hold of the bench and rushed out the door to the lobby where I found a water dispenser. "Whew, I made it. Thank you, God!"

As I was getting myself together to head back into the courtroom, I heard this voice. A voice that I once thought I loved but later feared and eventually began to hate. "Wow, look at you. Still sexy as hell just like I pictured you. It's been a while. I have been trying to contact you to check on you and our daughter but you're a hard one to keep up with. But hey, nothing is impossible. Remember that. I'll be out here soon, ready to take back what's mine, so be ready... oh, and tell that cornball you're dealing with, his time is up. Daddy's coming home!! That's a promise!!!"

Now, the old me would have been shaking in my boots but this did nothing but make me laugh. Did this fool really say this to me? In front of a live studio audience? Ha ha ha! This man has some serious issues. After fifteen years of being incarcerated, you would think that maybe... hopefully.. prayerfully, he would have matured or something but he still seems like the same mean, evil, revengeful Preston to me. Oh well, not my problem.

Sitting in that courtroom listening to and reliving that horrible day, almost sixteen years to the day, was so overwhelming. There were details that I never shared with anyone because it was something I wanted to forget. I did not want to go on the stand but I wrote a letter and my lawyer Mr. David Jones read it on my behalf.

"To whom it may concern,

Hello, my name is Tamara Lynnae Wilson and I am a survivor! On February 15, 2007, I was in the hospital and had just given birth to my beautiful daughter, two days prior. I was waiting to be released when I heard a whole bunch of chaos going on in the hallway.

I got up and grabbed my baby but before I could leave the room to the hallway, Preston and some female I had never seen before came into the room and Preston took the baby from my arms. I was yelling and I grabbed Preston's shoulder because I didn't want to do anything that could harm our daughter. That's when this female that came with him grabbed me from behind and she and Preston proceeded to jump on me, hitting me, and kicking me all while security and other staff tried to get them off of me.

Preston pulled a clear water bottle out of his jacket pocket and he tossed the "water" which hit two of the nurses and a security officer as he was rushing out the door (still holding my 2-day-old baby in his arm). The female who I later found out was his mistress at the time was also pregnant by him), grabbed the water bottle from Preston and began tossing it as she was backing out of the hospital room.

Thank God, they didn't make it out of the hospital with my baby girl. I suffered 2nd and 3rd degree burns to my neck, shoulders, and back as well as part of my face.

Innocent people were hurt by this horrible act. To this day, I still don't understand why this happened.

I am asking that Preston King sign over his rights to our daughter Alaina Marie King, so we can move on with our lives for good."

As my lawyer read the letter on my behalf, I watched as Preston listened with no emotion. He looked like he was getting pleasure hearing it. Up until he heard Mrs… then he showed the Preston that I knew. He stood up and started calling out all types of names that I would not repeat. He told me they should have killed me and taken my baby as they planned. He even told me how miserable he would make my life. He said he would find out who my husband was and he was going to make him regret stealing his family.

Oh, he showed his behind in that courtroom and I loved every bit of it. It made my case so much easier.

Well, I'll just say God is good. What the enemy took as evil, God turned into good!

Preston thought he could break me but what he did was help me get back to my first true love which is God.

I lost myself in a man because I didn't love myself. I allowed and put up with his abuse because I felt I was weak. I felt I had to. I didn't love myself. See, when you don't truly love yourself, you allow so much. Deep down, you know when you're settling, even if it's hard to admit. I'm here to tell you… you can move on. Self-love is very important. It's easy to say but hard to do. I suggest if you're feeling down on yourself, and feel like you don't deserve love, happiness, joy, or peace, I'm asking you to please seek help. Speak to someone. Most importantly. Talk to Jesus. He's the one that can truly help you.

You don't have to settle and deal with a person who doesn't respect you. Don't accept cheating, talking to you in any kind of way, or putting their hands on you. Most times, it starts with a push or mug, then they see they can get away with that, then it gets worse and it won't stop until you stop it or they kill you. Leave before it gets any worse. It's not worth losing your life over. Please talk to someone and get out! I did it and so can you! I am a survivor of domestic abuse!

CHAPTER 7

The Ultimate Betrayal

How in the world did I get here?" I guess I know now what it means when they say 'When a woman is fed up, there's no telling what she will do.'

I haven't had much sleep lately because I had so much on my mind. So many plans, emotions, and ideas just ran through my mind all night.

Well, last night I prayed so hard and asked the Lord to give me sweet sleep and He did just that. It felt so good. Tommy didn't come home again last night, so maybe that was another reason I slept so well. It seems like I get the best sleep on the nights when he stays out.

I don't know why whenever Tommy comes in from staying out all night, he always picks a fight with me. I'm so used to it, it's a part of his routine. For the most part, I just try to avoid him in every way possible.

This particular morning, I got up, took my shower, and got dressed for work. I got to work 10 minutes earlier than normal. I even had time to stop and buy donuts for everyone like I used to do. It felt so good.

I was sitting at my desk listening to my Gospel music. I needed my Jesus music (as they call it in the office).

I had my AirPods on and I was in my zone working. My desk phone rang, I quickly picked up the phone because it startled me. My phone's ringing volume was up to the max, so I'm sure everyone in the office heard it ring too! I answered the phone and there was a female on the line asking to speak to me. "May I ask who's calling and what is this in reference to?" I replied.

She then began to tell me who she was and why she was calling me. "Hey, girl, my name is Lakresha and I just want you to know I have been messing around with Tommy for six months now and I'm pregnant with his baby."

I responded as politely as possible. "Hello Lakresha, well, I guess congratulations are in order but I'm confused as to where you got my work number from and why are you calling me. All of this sounds like a personal issue between you and Tommy. I don't have anything to do with this." She started to cry and told me how ever since she told him about her pregnancy, he's been avoiding her calls and text messages. She has even been around my house a few times, hoping to run into him or me.

I explained to her that I was sorry about what she was going through but I was at work and I was not sure what she was expecting from me.

Although Tommy and I went through so much, I still loved him but I knew I needed to get away from him. This right here, was my final straw.

We have talked about having children together, so to find out he's having a child by someone else is heartbreaking but a blessing. I was taught a long time ago to keep my head up and never let them see me sweat.

I had to sit there at work for the rest of the day answering calls and looking into these people's faces smiling like everything was fine when in reality I wanted to go home, lock myself in my room, and cry my eyes out!

After I ended the phone call with Lakresha, I went into the bathroom on the 2nd floor. I locked myself in there and just cried. I didn't want to but I had to let it out. How could Tommy do this to me? This isn't the 1st time he cheated on me but he never brought a baby. The last time, I told him that I was getting tired of his cheating habit, and the next time he cheated on me again, I would leave him for good. I'm sure he didn't believe me but I have to stand by my word this time!

Tommy would just laugh it off and tell me neither one of us was going anywhere. I was going to be his wife and the mother of his children. He thought it was something I wanted or needed to hear but I didn't need or want to hear these lies. All I ever asked for or wanted was the truth!

For the remaining time of the day, I was trying to figure out how to handle this. Do I call him now and confront him or wait to do it face-to-face so that I can look into his eyes? When he lies, he does this thing with his left eye. He doesn't even know that I know when he's lying. I just don't say anything. Should I just leave without saying a word? Do I make him leave and I stay and change the locks? Do I just forgive him again and work it out? Do I go after the girl? Besides, who knows what he has been telling her about me? She's pregnant and what would be the point in doing that? She doesn't owe me anything. He does.

Honestly though, I had to ask myself, "What am I expecting from him?" This isn't the first time he cheated but this is the first time a female had the nerve to reach out to me. This has to be a deal breaker. I want out, right? Is this a sign from God showing me he's never going to change? It's a baby today, a disease tomorrow, what's after that? More babies, more drama? Uuugh my mind is all over the place. I did ask the Lord to show me a sign. Could this be the Lord confirming things to me? I just started praying. God doesn't work that fast! Or does He? Hmmmm? What I do know is time seems to be going extra slow. Feels like time stopped and took a few breaks. I still have two more hours before it's time to get out of there. The day continued to drag on until...

Finally, it's 4:30 and I'm off the clock! I got into my 2019 Impala and turned the radio on. They were playing the 80's old-school music, so that put me in a good headspace. I love the 80's music, good, clean, and fun music. It took my mind off of Tommy and his now maybe baby momma drama.

Thirty-six minutes later, I pulled up to my house, Tommy was nowhere to be found, again. I'm relieved and hurt at the same time. It's been almost two whole days since I last spoke to or even saw Tommy. We both are very stubborn, so I know he won't call me first, and for me to call or text him would be like me giving in and breaking, so that cannot happen.

I didn't want to share this information with anyone because I was too embarrassed. My friends have been telling me that I deserve better since the first month Tommy and I started dating.

One of my friends actually liked Tommy and that's Tina. Tina and I were like sisters. We had been friends since Pre-K. Our parents were best friends, so we pretty much grew up like sisters. She always told me I was being extra and that I needed to give Tommy a break.

Ok, so, here's the thing, Tommy was working when we first got together. He was the team leader in the IT department at a major pharmaceutical company. That's how we met. He was the man. He was very well put together. He looked good, smelled good, and was such a charmer. After flirting and small talk for about six months, he finally got the nerve to ask me out. It's been on and popping since. For the past two years, he's been working these little jobs here and there and doing the bare minimum as far as helping with household needs.

Anyway, I decided to call Lisa. She was acting a little weird like she was very short with me. I asked her if she was okay and she said, "Yes, I'm okay, just not sure why you are acting like everything is fine with you." I tried to play it off like I didn't know what she was talking about. What I was confused about was how in the world she heard about Tommy getting some tramp pregnant. She doesn't even know if it's true, so I am not trying to hear all of the speculations and the long-drawn-out lectures about how I deserve better, and how Tommy is a bum with nothing going for himself. I wasn't in the mood for that so I just cut her off and told her now is not the time.

I simply just said, "Listen, I heard the rumors but I haven't spoken to Tommy to confirm anything so until I hear it from his mouth, it's nothing but rumors, so I'd appreciate it if you don't bring it up or repeat it to anyone else. If you're my real friend you will respect my privacy, Lisa." She agreed and we changed the subject.

After going back and forth with myself about calling Tommy, I decided not to call or text him and to just wait. It's been two whole days now since he's been home and not even a text or phone call this time. Well, another good night's sleep for me.... so I thought.

Around 2:48 am, my phone started ringing. It was an unknown caller. I don't answer blocked calls especially not this time of the morning. I turned the phone over and went back to sleep.

Two minutes later, my phone was blowing up again. I thought I turned this ringer off (talking to myself), but before I could turn the phone completely off, it rang again back to back so I said this better be an emergency calling me this time of the morning back to back.

"Hello"

"Hi, this is Lakresha please don't hang up. I know this is so out of pocket for me to call you, especially since you don't know me and because of the situation we're in but I really need your help. I did something really bad and I don't know what to do."

"Listen La Keeda, LaKieesa, LaQueeta, or whatever your name is… it's two something in the morning and I was sleeping so peacefully. I can't believe I'm sitting here this long entertaining your stupid, home-wrecking behind anyway. What do you want from me? Listen trick, you slept or still sleeping with my man, then you call and tell me you're carrying his baby and also told me he's avoiding your calls, and now you're harassing me because you can't get in touch with my man? And I'm sitting here at 2:56 am entertaining all of this? What could you possibly want from me, girl? And why are you crying? I can't understand with all of that crying in my ear."

"l didn't mean it. I didn't mean to do it but he lied to me. He told me she was his sister and the whole time they have been sleeping together and I caught him!!" "He's a liar!" She said in the middle of tears.

"Ok, hold up, slow down (She got my attention now). The whole time I was thinking, OMG, this man has another woman? Yes, this is just what I needed to push me to move on. This is it. Three women during the same time? Oh no, I can't do this. Tommy, how could you do this to me? To us? Ugh, so many things going through my head that I got lost in my own thoughts and forgot I was on the phone with La whatever!

"Ok girl, spill it and make it quick please, so I can try to go back to sleep. Sooooooo, Tommy is cheating on us with somebody who you assumed was his sister?" Alright, so what does this have to do with me? If you want to know if I am going to leave him the answer is yes. You can have him. I'm done and y'all can share and enjoy each other. You got it. Y'all got what you wanted, right? Great... good night girl and please don't call me anymore," I said ready to hang up.

"Noooo, please don't hang up. Please. I have to get this out. I have been calling Tommy for months and he hasn't answered but he sent two guys to my place and they offered me $10,000 cash to get an abortion and to act like none of this ever happened. I took the money but I'm taking it and leaving the state. I'm keeping my son and making sure Tommy has nothing to do with him or me. " Lakresha explained.

"Listen, girl, this is your last freaking chance, what does any of this have to do with me?! Please get to the point or I'm hanging up, I promise you!" I yelled, pissed.

"I'm sorry, I'm sorry, well since he was ignoring me, I was angry, so I rode past his house and I saw two cars there, and then I ...

"Wait, wait, what do you mean you went to his house?" I asked.

"Yes, his house. He lives there with his sister. Well, who I thought was his sister, turned out to be his wife! Lakresha replied.

"Wait a minute, you must be talking about somebody else because #1, Tommy lives here with me, wait, no, #1, Tommy is not married. We are engaged but not married yet and Tommy does not have his own place. Have you ever been there? Where is "His place?" Please share (giggling because now you got my attention. Honey, you must have the wrong Tommy because none of this is correct. I am up and entertained at this point (In my head)." She really believed this man was married and had his own place... Poor Chile (chuckling inside)" $10,000??? Tommy?? Yeah, right. He's been working these corny jobs bringing home about $230 a week, where would he get $10,000 from??" I asked confused.

"Honey, it's public records. You can look it up yourself. Yes, he's married and he lives at 338 Jars Ave. He and his wife bought the house last May. They don't have any kids yet but they have been trying. She's having a hard time getting pregnant, so she has been to two different fertility doctors so far. They own a salon together as well. The name of the salon is "HAIR BEE IT" and it's on 745 East

Walnut Street...Lakresha continued to dish out more information before I interrupted her.

"Hold the heck up. Backtrack, rewind... what did you say the address was and the name of the salon?" I asked.

"His home address is 338 Jars Av and the salon address is 745 East Walnut Street. I looked that up too and I even sent flowers there for Tommy when I found this out and I wrote a letter to his wife telling her everything about Tommy and me. Instead of jumping on her husband, she called me a whore, a home wrecker and told me my bastard baby was going to die.

Well, she called me earlier today asking if we could meet up face-to-face at their salon. She said the three of us could work something out. I can't believe I fell for it. When I got there, there were two clients still there. She asked if I could give her a second, and asked if I needed anything to eat or drink. I mean she was very nice and it made me ease up a little. I'm not here to trash or bash this man. I just wanted the respect that my son and I deserve. I was not a quick one-night stand and I refused to let Tommy act like I was."

"Look, Chile, I am not your therapist. Time is ticking!" I replied.

Lakresha continued with her narration."Well, anyway, when her last client left, here comes like three people out of nowhere and they started hitting, punching, kicking and just beating on me. I just balled up trying to protect my baby boy and that's when I heard Tommy's voice. He said, "See, if only you would have just taken the money; but no, you want to be a dummy and try to control me and trap me with a baby. Then, he said, "Damn Bae, we should have just finished her and taken that baby.

At this point, I'm still balled up on the cold marble floors, filthy from her last two client's hair all over me, crying, scared, confused, and praying that the Lord will get my baby and me out of there, safe.

In the midst of my thoughts, I remembered I brought my gun just in case of an emergency. Thankfully I had my pocketbook strapped around me so it was easy to access. As I'm balled up holding my belly, my pocketbook is tucked under as well to protect my belly.

I reached into my pocketbook and came out and I just started shooting not caring who or what I hit. I just knew I had to get out of here alive. I remember firing the first shot and after that, everything went blank and when I got into my car, I didn't call the police instead I called you. I don't know why I called you but please help me. I am scared. I could have killed somebody. A couple of people. I just don't know what to do. Can you please help me? If I go to jail, could you please take my son? Please. I don't want them to take my son from me, please. I'm begging you." Lakresha pleaded between tears.

Hold up…hold up, that address she gave me is my best friend Lisa's address and that is Lisa's shop. She got her information all jacked up. But wait, did she say she shot somebody at my best friend's shop? Wait, hold up, what's going on here? All of this is going on in my head. I finally stopped her ranting and asked, "Where are you?" "I am sitting in my car around the corner from the shop. Please help me. I am scared. I should have never gone there. I should have accepted the fact I would be a single mom and just moved on," Lakresha said.

[In my head, I'm still so confused because those addresses she gave me were to my best friend Lisa's house and her salon] " So, I'm being honest with you. I'm trying to figure out what's going on but I'm telling you right now if I find out this is some sort of prank and you got me up out of my bed running around like a little flunky, I'm beating you down personally, pregnant or not and I mean it!" I threatened her.

"I promise I am not lying to you, I told you I don't know why I called you. I really don't know why but yes, it's Lisa. He told me she was his sister. They live together. I have been there to the house with them plenty of times. She cooked and we had dinner together. She even had male friends come over when I was there, so I never thought anything.

I told him they seemed really close to be brother and sister but hey, it was never anything too crazy, I just felt he was a little too overprotective but now I see why. I just don't get it. Why would they do this to me? He told me he loved me and everything. He told me we were going to get married and have kids. He really made me believe he loved me. I can't believe this. I can't believe I may have shot somebody." Lakresha cried.

I cannot believe I am really up and putting clothes on to go help this lady, I don't even know, who just so happens to be "pregnant " by my man. Really God?? Is this what we are doing??

I can't believe this but I told her to send me her location and give me a minute.

As I was sitting up on the side of my bed putting my shoes on, in my head again, I was like wait... is this a setup?? She could be trying to set me up and I'm walking right into it.

I didn't even think about this before but I called Tommy's phone. No answer. I call Lisa's phone. Straight to her voicemail. I decided to call the salon and after two rings someone picked up the phone.

"Hello? Hello? Is anyone there?" Said an unfamiliar voice. I couldn't speak or say anything. I don't know why I didn't just hang right up but the male on the other end of the phone had a raspy deep voice and he said, "Hello??? This is Officer Barrette." I slammed the phone down and called Lakresha and told her to meet me at the Dunkin Donuts on Marshall St which is around the corner from the shop.

As I was on the phone with Lakresha, I could hear the sirens so loud like they were coming my way. As I was grabbing my keys to leave my house, my phone started ringing.

Me: (before I even thought) "Hello?"

Officer Barrette: (caller on the other line) "Hello? Hi, this is Officer Barrett you called this number a few minutes ago and I wanted to ask you a few questions. Do you mind answering a few questions please?"

Me: "Well, I was sleeping. What is this in reference to?"

Officer Barrett: "Ma'am can you please come to the police station and answer a few questions? You can either meet us there or we can come and pick you up and bring you in. The choice is yours but we definitely need to ask you some questions."

Me: "Well I guess I have no choice. I will meet you there but officer I don't know what is going on."

Officer Barrett: Thank you ma'am and see you soon. [Hangs up phone]

I was still on the phone with Lakresha, "Okay, girl, this is what you're going to do. I'm coming to pick you up and we're going to go to the police station and you're going to tell them exactly what you told me. You are going to be fine. I can't believe I'm saying this but I'll call my lawyer tomorrow and see if you have a case and I'll see if she will represent you."

(Lakresha still crying, even harder now) "Omg, thank you so much. I was so scared. I never thought I would have to use my gun. I can't lie though, I have to be honest with you. When I heard Tommy's voice I imagined myself shooting him because he really hurt me. Tommy was my everything. I didn't know about you. I thought I was the only one. I thought we were building for our future. I'm carrying his son. His first and only child whom we talked about sharing and raising as a young black king and that we would name him 'KING' that way he would never forget who he is... a king who was born to the Most High King (Jesus).

I don't know what lies he told you as well or even how long you two have been dealing with each other but I'm sorry you're going through this as well. We don't deserve this."

As I was pulling up to her, I could see the lights flashing, the police cars all up the block, two ambulances still there, and one already on its way to one of the local hospitals. I guess I'm still in shock because normally, I would be running to make sure my bestie, my sister, my road dawg, my comforter, my other half was good, and even my man, my protector, my lover, my other best friend, my hero. Instead, I'm running the darn streets at 4:25 am to help a home-wrecking, pregnant stranger who was sleeping with my man (well her man now). Something gotta be wrong with me Lord!

I said to Lakresha, "Come on, girl, get in this car!"

As we are in the car talking, I learn so much about my best friend Lisa and my man Tommy. This La kre kre chick isn't so bad after all. I'm actually feeling her pain and feeling bad for her. I mean, don't get me wrong. I do love Tommy but I was over him and the controlling, manipulation, the lies, not coming home, him getting drunk and picking fights, like, I was over it. I stuck around so long because I just didn't feel like moving on and starting over. I just figured he would get better but it didn't. I just got numb.

We got to the police station and Officer Barrett let me know upfront I was not a suspect but because I called the salon at that time of the morning, it sent red flags because there was a possible robbery and shooting there hours before.

I introduced Lakresha to Officer Barrett and told him she would explain what happened.

She told Officer Barrett and his crew exactly what she told me. They then let us know that Lisa was shot in her arm, Tommy was shot in his butt and left thigh and another female named Kris was grazed in the shoulder, so thank God nobody died and Kree Kree won't be going down for murder. Her gun was registered and the police took and viewed the surveillance cameras and confirmed crazy Kree Kree's story!

Lakresha turned out to be a really cool chick. She moved to Rhode Island with a family member and two months later, she had her son. A healthy baby boy whom she named King. My godson. Yeah, I know, right? As for Lisa and Tommy, they survived and are still together and no longer a part of my life and I couldn't be more happy.

CHAPTER 8

WIND

Good morning gorgeous. I see you're finally up. How are you feeling this morning? Ready to get something to eat yet? Come on, get up and get yourself together. I'll come back and get you in about fifteen minutes. Hello? Miss Grayham? Can you hear me?"

Breakfast was slamming. I had turkey bacon, scrambled eggs with green peppers and onions, hash browns, grits, hot tea Chai flavor, and also a glass of orange juice. This place is really cool and the staff is amazing. All of the ladies I met here so far have been really kind and encouraging. I was given a packet that included the house rules, services they offer, programs I must complete, and it even has counselors on site. This place is amazing. The one thing I don't care for is being away from my family but I was able to reach out to them from a burner cell phone they gave me in my package. The phone is just to let your loved ones know you're safe but they cannot know where you are because of the risk of your abuser finding you.

I went back to my room, about to get myself together and start the rest of my day and then I got this sharp pain in my abdomen. Then another one! and another one!!! Before I knew it, fluid was all over the floor and my contractions were coming like 3-4 minutes apart. I yelled, "Somebody please help me!" The pains were unbearable.

Dr. Felisha, the in-house midwife was amazing. She made it so much easier for me to deliver my healthy baby boy. I named him John after my father who was an upright man. What a great honor to name my son John Arthur.

I was only at this place for a few weeks but I was adapting to "my new life" and I can honestly say I am very happy. I feel safe. The ladies and children here have become like my family. Mrs. Tarah the owner of the facility is hands on and I really like that. When I say she goes above and beyond to make you feel welcome and make sure all of your needs are met that's an understatement.

Everyone in the house was really nice but out of everyone there, I instantly connected with Seymone. She was a 38-year-old mother of three who had been in an abusive relationship for over ten years. Like so many of us, she tried to leave several times and he always convinced her he was sorry and wouldn't do it again. "How many times have we heard this? "

Mondays and Thursdays were the days the counselors had what they call "open sessions," it's for the group. You don't need to sign up or do anything. The counselors are there to support all of your needs.

Kendra and Leah are Seymones sisters, they reached out to the facility and got their sister and her children away from Derrick, her abusive husband.

Things were finally looking up for both myself and Seymone. She was about to move into a 3-bedroom home and I would be right behind her in a few months.

Seymone was excited because she went back to nursing school and Mrs. Tarah put her in contact with someone in the hospital so while in school, she was also working part-time.

I was so proud of us. Life was really looking up. Until one day, Seymone didn't make it to work. We received a call that Seymone did a no-call no-show at work that day. We all knew that was not normal for her.

I instantly went to check on her kids. They were all in their classes safe and protected. This was the longest day ever. Everyone has been calling around trying to find out what happened to Seymone. "Where could she be?" Everyone asked.

We later found out Seymone had a weak moment and she reached out to Derrick. He pleaded and told her how much he loved and missed her. Not once did he mention or ask about the kids which should have been the biggest red flag but she agreed to meet up so they could talk. Seymone knew in her heart this was a mistake but she felt she needed closure. She needed to know for sure if she was over this so-called relationship and over Derrick for good this time. She saw how far she and her children had gotten without him.

As Seymone pulled up to the restaurant, she sat in the car and debated if this was what she really wanted to do. She changed her mind and called Derrick to let him know she had a change of plans, she just pulled off and headed to work. What she did not do was to pay attention to her surroundings which she was reminded of at WIND constantly. One not-so-smart move could mess you up big time and unfortunately, that was Seymone's story.

Derrick followed her as she was getting out of her 4-door, teal blue Honda Accord in the parking lot. Derrick came from behind her and strangled Seymone and left her lifeless body right there like she was a piece of trash.

How could he do this to the mother of his children? What about the babies?? Why would he do this? He's such a coward.

Can you believe this coward tried to say it was self-defense? He said that Seymone attacked him and he was only defending himself. Needless to say, Derrick will be spending the rest of his miserable life behind bars and I am now a mother of four, raising my best friends' children.

Today is my move-in day. I am so excited. I am so thankful for WIND (Women In New Direction), they have given me a fresh start in life. I met a group of women with whom we have grown together and built a sisterhood. A bond that can't be broken. I just wish Seymone could have been here to celebrate with the rest of us. Seymone was brought to WIND three weeks before I got there. She was the first woman I instantly clicked with. We became like sisters. Her positivity made me believe this was the best thing for me. She even helped me get back to my first love which is Christ. I'm grateful for our bond, and "sisterhood-ship" as we called it.

ABOUT THE AUTHOR

My name is Tara(h) Newby. I was born and raised in Norristown PA where I grew up in the home with both of my parents and my three beautiful older sisters. I come from a huge family on both sides. My mom was one of six children. Five daughters and one son. My father was the oldest of sixteen. Ten sons and six daughters.

I was blessed with three biological children, eight bonus children, and a total of sixteen grandchildren with two bonus grandchildren.

Nov 1, 2011, I married my Job Corps sweetheart Damion Newby. Whew, I am so thankful for this man.

I am an active member of Tabernacle Harvest Church in Pottstown PA, where God's favor reigns! My Pastors are Brian and Crystal Weatherspoon.

What I enjoy the most is spending time with my loved ones. Family means so much to me.

Help Is Available

National Domestic Violence Hotline

https: www.thehotline.org/get-help/domestic

800-799-7233

National Resources Center on Domestic Violence

www.ncadv.org

800-537-2238

The Women's Center of Montgomery County:

2506 N Broad St

Suite 203 Colmar, Pa 18915

(215)996-0723

1(800)773-2424

www.Wcmontco.org